D0106885

If Wishes Were Horses

by Bernadette Kelly

STONE ARCH BOOKS
a capstone imprint

First published in the United States in 2010
by Stone Arch Books
A Capstone Imprint
151 Good Counsel Drive, P.O. Box 669
Mankato, Minnesota 56002
www.capstonepub.com

First published in Australia by Black Dog Books in 2006

Library of Congress Cataloging-in-Publication Data is available on
the Library of Congress website.

Library Binding: 978-1-4342-1929-9

Art Director: Kay Fraser
Graphic Designer: Emily Harris
Production Specialist: Michelle Biedscheid
Photo Credit: Capstone Studio/Karon Dubke, cover

If Wishes Were Horses

by Bernadette Kelly

My life has changed so much over the past year. Sometimes I can't believe it. I wake up in the morning, look at the sun coming up past the Japanese maple growing outside my window, and I feel like I'm in a dream.

Just a year ago, I would have woken up to smog and horns honking, the noise of the city all around me. Now it's country silence, or the gentle sounds of the horses in my neighbors' paddocks, their hooves pounding on the ground.

Of course, a year ago, when my father decided that our family was moving to Ridgeview, it seemed more like a nightmare. On moving day, the only thing that got me through was thinking that maybe I'd get a horse of my own now that we were moving to the country.

Things are great now. But they didn't always seem so perfect.

I pulled down the last horse poster from my bedroom wall. My eyes swept the room. The place looked bigger, now that all the furniture was gone. The walls glowed white and bare without their decorations.

In the rectangular space where the bed had been, the carpet looked different. It was soft and new-looking next to the worn carpet patch around it, where I had stomped back and forth over the years.

The large bedroom window stared into the street like a giant eye. Behind the glass pane, a million glittering city lights danced and winked in a black night sky. Floating among the lights, my pale reflection gazed back at me.

I wasn't sure how I was supposed to feel at this moment. The city was no longer my home. Now it was just a place I would visit on special occasions, to eat at a fancy restaurant with Mom and Dad or see my friends.

It felt weird to be leaving the apartment for the last time. I was moving away from everything I had ever known.

I knew my mother had mixed feelings about this move too. A month ago, in July, my dad had been offered a new job with a real estate agent in the small country town of Ridgeview. My mother had been happy for him, but she'd also been concerned about the changes it would bring.

"What about Annie's school, Rob? And my teaching job. What about our friends?" she'd asked.

"But what an opportunity, Susan," my father had said. "A new life in the country, with fresh air and room to move. Think of the space. We can buy a big house, maybe on a few acres. You can have that vegetable garden you've always wanted. Ridgeview has a good school for Annie, and you can work there. In fact, I looked into it. They have an opening for a math and science teacher. It's perfect for you. As for our friends, they can all come and visit whenever they want."

"It sounds like you've thought of everything," said my mother sadly.

Of course my father had won. He always did. And now here we were, about to start a whole new life. New house. New school. New friends.

Leaving my city friends behind was hard.

What if I didn't fit in at the new school?

What if I didn't find a friend?

What if the kids thought I was a stuck-up city kid?

Even worse, what if I didn't like any of them?

I thought about the last time I saw my friends. I'd expected my friends to be at least a little sad about me leaving. But everyone was excited about a party coming up that weekend. They'd said goodbye in a wave of giggles and excited chatter.

My best friend, Jade O'Brien, was the only one who seemed to care. She was horrified when I told her that Ridgeview didn't have a movie theater. Worse still, it didn't even have a decent mall.

"What do you mean they don't have a mall?" demanded Jade. "How do they eat? Buy magazines? Buy clothes? What do they do for fun?"

"They have a few stores," I explained. "Just not like the stores we're used to. There's definitely not anything like Kundle Mall."

That was the mall where Jade and I liked to hang out. All of our friends hung out there on weekends and after school. There was nothing like that in Ridgeview.

"But what about Dippin' Donuts? Girlz Scene? Book Time?" Jade asked. "Is there at least a movie theater?"

I just shook my head.

"Annie, you can't exist without those stores. It's just . . . it's just not right. You could report your parents for child abuse or something. They're . . . they're being so selfish."

Jade looked so outraged that I had to laugh. Privately I agreed with my friend. And yet, it just didn't feel right to agree out loud.

"Hey, it's not all bad," I said. "My new bedroom is almost twice the size of my old one. I won't have to put up with Mrs. Fraser's bad music from upstairs. And I get out of drama class with Mr. Trope — which has to be a good thing."

Jade smiled, but still looked unconvinced.

"And we'll have way more room," I went on. "We have lots of land. Which means I can finally get a horse. I'll have plenty to do with a horse to ride and take care of. I'm not going to have time to miss . . . everything here."

It was true that my dad had always said he would love to buy me a horse. "But it just isn't practical," he would often explain. "There's no way you can have a horse in the city."

My secret dream of owning a horse was the one thing that made moving to the country okay. I hadn't run the idea past my parents yet, but nothing was standing in my way of getting a horse. Not now.

"A horse?" Jade's eyes narrowed. "Since when are you getting a horse, Annie?"

My uneasy stomach began doing somersaults.

"Jade O'Brien, are you calling me, your best friend, a liar?" I asked. My stomach was making me feel sick.

"Hey, no. It's just . . . this is the first time I've heard about it," Jade said quickly.

"Okay, so maybe I won't get it right away. But I'll definitely have a horse by the end of summer vacation," I said, my stomach flipping. "By the time you see me again, I'll be the best rider in Ridgeview."

Jade shrugged. "Well, who am I going to sit next to in class?" she said, changing the subject.

* * *

I glanced down at the poster in my hands. It was an old glossy photo of a dazzling Arabian horse, decked out in a full traditional costume.

I loved horses. Any size, any breed. I had only ridden a horse once, at camp.

My horse had been a dusty old bay with a white blaze down his face. The horse's name was Toby. I could still remember the feeling of bliss I'd had as I sat in the saddle and stroked his neck.

Other than that, the only horses I knew were the police horses. I knew quite a few of the mounted police officers who patrolled the city. I had often taken the chance to approach them and chat, spending precious moments stroking their horses. The police officers were always nice to me if they didn't have anything to do, and sometimes they'd teach me stuff about horses.

My whole life depended on having a horse. It might even help me make new friends. Without a horse, a lonely, boring summer vacation stretched out before me.

I would have to talk to my dad — get him at the right moment. He had to agree. He just had to.

"Annie," Mom called from the living room, shaking me from my thoughts. "Time to go."

My mother held a framed family photo that had been left hanging on the wall. Mom stuffed the frame into her handbag.

It didn't fit. More than half of the frame poked out of her bag.

I could see my father's bearded face staring back at me from the photo. I'd been told my own brown eyes and dark hair were identical to his. My mother's blue eyes and fair features were buried in the handbag.

My mother and I closed our apartment door for the last time. As I climbed into our car's back seat, my dog's paws greeted me.

Jonesy had been my birthday present a few years ago. He was a purebred Jack Russell terrier and still acted like a puppy. We adored each other. But I still wanted a horse — not as a pet, but as a companion. I hoped Jonesy wouldn't be jealous.

Jonesy settled down as soon as the car began to move. He opened his mouth wide and yawned.

That made me yawn too. I wondered if my bed would be ready to climb into at the new house. The moving truck hadn't arrived until lunchtime. Now, the sun had already set, and we'd been busy all day.

Dad had followed the truck in his car. He wanted to be at the house when our boxes were unloaded.

My father was like that. He said he liked to be prepared. My mom said he liked to organize everything and everybody.

My mother and I had stayed at the apartment to clean after everything was moved out. Now we were leaving for the long drive to Ridgeview.

"Excited?" my mother asked.

"Hmmm," I answered with another yawn.

"Get some sleep, sweetie. I'll wake you up when we get there."

I glanced at Jonesy. The dog's head rested lazily on his paws and his eyelids were closed.

I settled back into the seat as Mom started the car and we drove away.

I imagined the conversation I would have with my father — the conversation about getting a horse. I had some really good reasons for being allowed to have a horse. I fell asleep before I could imagine my father's reply.

I woke up the next morning in my old bed
in my new bedroom. We had arrived late in
the night to find only our beds put together.
That was fine, because I had no energy to do
anything except crawl into bed.

I looked around at my new surroundings.
Boxes containing all my possessions covered
the floor. The room was twice the size of my
old one, with a huge closet taking up one
of the walls. Everything looked strange and
unfamiliar.

My large bedroom window looked out over the five-acre property on the outskirts of Ridgeview.

Dad had fallen in love with the place just three months ago. He'd purchased the house without my mother and me even seeing the place.

Luckily, I liked it too. My room was nice and big, with lots of wall space for my posters. Summer sunlight streamed into my room, filtered by the branches of a Japanese maple that grew just a few yards from the house.

I looked at the oval-shaped corral beyond the yard and chewed my lip thoughtfully. Except for the chirps and whistles of the birds outside, my surroundings were quiet.

At home there would be traffic noise, doors slamming, and engines starting up as people in the neighboring apartments left for work.

Then I remembered. This was home now. We weren't going back to the city.

I tried to look on the bright side. There was that paddock outside. With all this space in our new home, there were possibilities . . . definitely possibilities.

I heard my mother and father moving around in the kitchen. Breakfast smells wafted down the hall and settled in my nostrils. I smelled eggs and bacon. Someone must have sifted through the chaos and unpacked the box with all of our kitchen tools and dishes.

My stomach growled. Time to eat.

I bounced out of bed and pulled a sweatshirt over my pajamas. Then I hurried down the hall to the kitchen.

"Good morning, Annie." My mother placed a plate of steaming eggs and toast in front of me.

My dad was already at the table eating as Mom and I sat down.

"Well, here we all are!" he announced. "You're a lucky girl, Annie. You've got the whole summer to get to know this place."

"Dad —" I began.

"You can make a few friends before school starts," Dad told me. "I wish I had more than just a few days before I start work. I'll have to drive into town today. My boss told me about a woman who breeds sheep. Now that we have all this extra land, we'll need some animals to keep the grass short."

My face fell. "Sheep? Nobody told me we were getting sheep."

My father laughed. "I know," he told me. "Your mother and I wanted to surprise you. Imagine how much fun you'll have taking care of them. And there will be lambs soon, too!"

I stared at my father. He looked so pleased with himself. Standing behind him, my mother raised one eyebrow and shrugged.

As usual, my mom would go along with whatever my dad wanted. Nothing was going like I'd planned it. How was I going to tell my father that I wasn't interested in sheep? I had my own plans for keeping the grass short.

"But Dad, I . . ." I couldn't go on. I stared sadly down at my eggs.

My mother touched me lightly on the arm and said, "What's the matter, sweetie?"

My father looked puzzled. "Come on, Annie. What's up?"

I took a deep breath. This wasn't how I'd planned my talk.

"Well . . . you see . . . I was hoping we could get a horse to keep the grass short," I said timidly.

"But you don't even know how to ride." My mother looked puzzled. "What do you know about taking care of a horse?"

I shrugged. "I could learn. I've always loved horses. You know that, Mom."

"Listen, Annie," my father interrupted. "It's one thing to collect horse posters. It's another to take on the responsibility of owning one. Believe me, Annie, you don't want a horse."

When my father spoke again, it was as if horses had never been mentioned.

"The sheep I have in mind are a special breed," he told me. "Apparently they're easy to take care of, and they never need shearing. With your mother and I both working, the last thing we need are animals that require a lot of work. And the best part about the whole thing is that we can sell the lambs when they're old enough. Then we'll make some money, too."

My mother looked thoughtful. "Rob, maybe we could think about the horse idea. Annie would be the one taking care of it, not us."

I turned my attention to my mother. "That's right. You wouldn't have to do a thing," I said. "Mom, you had a horse when you were younger."

Before my mother could answer, my father said, "Annie, I'm afraid I'm going to have to say no to a horse. I put a lot of time and effort into researching the sheep. I basically already bought them. I can't call their owner back and say, 'Sorry, I don't want your sheep now. My daughter's getting a horse instead.'"

I didn't see why my father couldn't do that. I didn't see how he could care more about some stranger's feelings than his own daughter's. But I knew my dad could be stubborn. No. Actually, my dad was always stubborn.

It reminded me of the time we'd painted my room at the old apartment.

Mom had promised me that I could pick out the colors I liked. I had my heart set on a very pale purple, with darker purple around the windowsills.

My father had shaken his head when I told him.

"No, Annie." He said the words slowly, as if I were three years old. "We should keep the color neutral. Neutral colors are always in style."

I didn't care one bit about neutral paint colors — I wanted purple. But before my mother and I could make a trip to the paint store, my father came home with an enormous can of plain, boring white paint. He painted the walls of my room that weekend. And that was that. End of discussion.

I finished my breakfast in silence. My mother washed the dishes. Finally, my father stood up from the table. "Well, I'm off to town."

I felt my dreams of having a horse disappear with him as he slammed the back door.

My disappointment soon turned into angry energy.

After I finished breakfast, I returned to my room. I thought about doing some unpacking, but suddenly, my room felt small and I felt trapped.

I dug through boxes until I found my favorite outfit. I pulled on a skirt, white sandals, and a white tank top, then ran a comb through my short hair and washed my face.

At the last minute, I grabbed my cell phone and slipped it into my skirt pocket. Then I headed back to the kitchen. My mom was putting dishes into the cupboard. There were empty boxes all around her.

"I'm taking Jonesy for a walk," I told my mother.

"Now?" my mother asked nervously. She looked out the window. "Maybe I should come with you."

"Don't worry, Mom. I promise I won't go far. I just want to take a look around."

My mother looked distracted. "Fine. But don't be gone longer than an hour. You still need to unpack." Her tone softened. "Are you okay?" she asked.

I nodded. "I'm fine," I answered quietly, but I wasn't. My chances of getting a horse had gone down to zero.

I tried not to think about it as Jonesy raced around my feet. I clipped on his leash. Then I stepped out the front door.

Our new property was named Hillgrove. It was on a corner, with tall pine trees growing in a ruler-straight line along the roadside boundary.

The whole neighborhood had once been a sprawling farm owned by just one family. Long ago, the farm had been split into small lots of five and ten acres.

There were neighbors on either side of our new house. I could see across the paddock into their yards. As I led an excited Jonesy along the driveway, I watched a blue SUV leaving the driveway of the house next door.

It looked like the people who lived there had horses. The backyard had a small fenced area with a stable attached. There was a horse trailer parked near the fence.

I could just make out a set of bright red and white show jumps on the far side of their house. There was no sign of a horse. Jealously, I wondered where it was.

Jonesy and I turned onto the street. There were no sidewalks, just a grassy path littered with leaves. The path wandered along beside the road.

I turned left. Turning right would mean turning the corner and having to pass the horse-loving neighbor's house. I wasn't up to meeting the horse owner today. I couldn't take the jealousy.

The hot sun beat down on my bare shoulders. I should have turned back for some sunscreen, but I didn't feel like it.

Jonesy was excited to explore his new surroundings. He tugged eagerly at his leash, forcing me to walk faster. Every property I passed had a leafy, tree-lined driveway with a mailbox at the gate. Many of the properties had names on the front gate, like "Serenity" and "Pineview."

Even though there were a lot of houses in my neighborhood, it was very quiet. The only sounds were my footsteps on the path and an occasional birdcall.

I could easily have been alone in the middle of nowhere. There was no traffic and no people.

Jonesy choked as he pulled his leash in excitement. I bent down to unclasp the leash. It was something I would never have done in the city, but here there was no traffic to run Jonesy over. The dog yapped excitedly and ran ahead.

I had to walk faster now to keep up with Jonesy. When he left the road and ran under a farm gate, I decided it was time to put him back on his leash.

"Jonesy! Here, boy," I called.

Jonesy ignored me. He picked up speed and headed across the paddock. I could make out a boundary fence, and, beyond that, a thick forest.

I needed to catch Jonesy quickly. If he ran into the forest I'd never find him.

The steel gate was tied securely with wire. I wasted a few minutes trying to unwind the wire. Finally, I gave up. I climbed the gate, tearing my skirt as it snagged on the wire.

To make matters worse, I banged my knee on the top of the gate and half-fell into the paddock on the other side.

Angry now, I called the dog again. "Jonesy, you crazy dog. Come here, now!"

Jonesy was now a white speck on the far side of the paddock. He had his nose to the ground and pretended he hadn't heard me.

I took off, running across the grass in my sandals.

I stopped when I stepped in something soft and wet, and my shoe came right off my foot. I stared down at the ground in disbelief. My favorite white shoe was stuck in the middle of a pile of fresh, green manure.

"Great!" I muttered. "That's just what I need right now."

Scowling, I bent down, trying desperately to find a clean part of my manure-covered shoe to grab.

I didn't see or hear the large animal approach from behind me.

When I turned around and looked up, I screamed. Standing right in front of me was the owner of the mess I'd stepped in. A black and white cow stared at me silently, flicking away flies with its tail.

Hopping on one leg and carefully holding a corner of the shoe, I was stuck. I was scared to move, afraid that the cow might chase me.

Worse, I could no longer see any sign of Jonesy. He had disappeared under the fence and into the woods.

What were you supposed to do when faced with a huge, terrifying cow? Were you supposed to stare into the cow's eyes? Or maybe just look at the ground and edge away slowly?

As I tried to figure out what to do, the cow lost interest and walked away.

I waited for my knees to stop trembling, and then tried to walk wearing only one shoe. But I soon discovered more than green grass growing in the paddock.

With every step, my foot found another sharp prickle that stuck into my skin. Wrinkling my nose in disgust, I dropped the smelly, manure-stained shoe to the ground and slipped my foot into it.

I finally reached the fence and peered into the forest beyond, but there was no sign of my little white dog. I felt a lump of panic rise from my stomach to my throat.

I checked my watch. My mother would start to worry if I wasn't home soon. I grabbed my phone, but then realized I didn't know my new phone number.

I knew that I should go back home and alert my mother, but I couldn't just leave Jonesy. Thinking about him, I felt so worried.

My poor sweet dog! He'd be so scared when he realized he was alone. I slipped through the wire fence strands and into the forest.

Once I left the paddock, the light dimmed almost immediately. The trees on either side closed in and blocked out the sun.

The leaves on the ground rustled as I moved through them. Small birds hopped in the leaves, but I was too distracted to notice them.

"Jonesy! Jonesy! Come here, boy!" I called out loudly.

Jonesy didn't appear. I started thinking about all the bad things that could happen to a small dog in the forest. A city dog that wouldn't know to stay away from animal traps. Or wild animals. Were there any wild animals in this forest?

I had been searching for ten long, awful minutes when I heard excited barking.

"Jonesy!" I called.

Something was moving in my direction, but it didn't sound like Jonesy. I wasn't sure what it was. It was crashing loudly through the forest. I could hear twigs snapping and a steady rustling.

It sounded like something much larger than a small, lightweight Jack Russell dog. But the closer it came, the closer Jonesy's barking seemed.

Then I heard a yell.

Chapter Four

A girl on a gray horse came into view. She was struggling to keep her agitated horse under control. I could tell right away why the horse was upset.

"Jonesy!" I yelled. I ran toward my dog, who yapped madly at the heels of the horse. The horse kicked, narrowly missing the dog with its hooves.

"Don't run," the girl told me in an angry tone. "You'll only upset him more."

I stopped running but kept my eye on Jonesy. "Come on, boy. Come here. Come on."

Jonesy looked up at me as if seeing me for the first time. He stopped barking and gave me a "look what I brought you" expression. It almost made me want to laugh, except that I was so mad at him for running away and scaring me.

I edged closer and lunged at the dog. I landed on my knees, but managed to catch Jonesy's back end.

The dog, barking again, struggled to escape. I closed my hands firmly around him and held tight.

I turned my attention back to the girl. The horse's neck was dark with sweat, but he stood quietly now that Jonesy was under control.

The girl patted her horse. "It's all right, Jefferson. It's okay, boy," she said quietly. Then she looked down at me. "What is wrong with that dog? Hasn't it ever seen a horse before?" she said sharply.

"I'm really sorry." I was mortified. "He got away from me. He's never been outside the city before. Everything's new for him, and he just got a little over-excited."

"Just a little? He should have been on a leash. It's against the law to just let your dog run around like that, you know," the girl said, looking annoyed.

I felt close to tears. The knee I had banged on the gate was throbbing. "I just let him off to run," I explained. "Then he got away from me. He's not used to all of the freedom, I guess. I really am sorry."

"Well, you'd have been a whole lot sorrier if he'd hurt Jefferson or me. I could have been thrown off, you know," she said.

The girl looked me up and down. I was still clutching Jonesy in my arms.

I suddenly became aware of my own appearance. My white tank top was now filthy. My light, flimsy skirt was torn. My shoes were all dusty, and one of them was covered in manure.

"You're definitely not from around here, are you?" asked the rider. "Are you from the new family that bought Hillgrove?"

I clipped the leash back onto Jonesy's collar and held out my hand. "That's right. My name's Annie Boyd."

"Well, Annie Boyd, just keep that dog away from my horse," the rider ordered.

Then she gathered up her reins and rode away.

I watched her leave, my hand still raised in mid-air.

When I arrived home, I had some explaining to do. I told my mother about Jonesy running away and the cow and the gate that I had to jump over.

I left out the part about the girl on the horse. Just thinking about it made me cringe. I knew my mother would be anxious if she thought I was upsetting one of our new neighbors. Besides, I was already in trouble for ripping my skirt, getting sunburned shoulders, and letting Jonesy off his leash.

I spent the rest of the day unpacking boxes, hanging up posters, and making my room my own.

My father came home around noon and was soon busy moving furniture and unpacking boxes, all the while talking about his plans to dig a vegetable garden.

I was still angry with my father. If he noticed, he chose to ignore it.

I hadn't given up on owning a horse.

Once we had settled into Ridgeview, I told myself, anything was possible. I wasn't going to let my father ruin my dream.

By the time my dad started work at
Ridgeview Real Estate a few days later, there
were still no sheep at Hillgrove.

I kept expecting a sheep-filled truck to
arrive. I was curious, but there was no way I'd
ask my dad about it. He might get the wrong
idea if I showed any interest in the sheep.

After a few days, I was sick of just hanging
around the house. I called Jade a few times,
but she never seemed to be home.

My mother suggested that I could help with the vegetable garden, but I preferred to explore my new neighborhood. I never let Jonesy off his leash again, and the forest land around my new home quickly became familiar.

Soon, I decided that comfort was more important than fashion. Instead of wearing skirts and cute tops and sandals, I walked in sneakers and wore sunscreen and clothes that covered me from the sun.

I found a path that led straight into the forest from the road, which meant I could avoid the cows. Inside the woods, there were dozens of paths.

My father told me that it was all part of a state park. He said that each path would eventually come out on the edges of the town of Ridgeview.

Jonesy and I explored each new path we came across. I hadn't gone all the way to town yet, but I soon felt completely familiar with my surroundings and could easily find my way back home.

Since that first disastrous day, I had not seen the girl from the forest again. I had figured out where she lived, though. The very same gray horse the girl had been riding grazed in the paddock next door to my house, where I had seen the horse trailer and show jumps that first day.

Jefferson grazed peacefully in the paddock, but there was no sign of life from the house. Despite the bad beginning, I really hoped that the girl and I would become friends.

Jonesy was good company, but he couldn't talk. I was starting to get really sick of my own voice.

Summer vacation stretched out before me. Without someone to hang out with, life was just boring. If I hadn't been feeling so nervous about going to a new school, I'd be looking forward to school starting, just because I was bored.

About a week after my encounter with the girl in the woods, there was a knock at my front door.

A woman and a girl were standing on the step. It took me a moment to realize that the girl was none other than the rider of the gray horse.

When we'd met, the girl had been wearing jodhpurs, boots, and a helmet that covered all of her hair. Today she wore pale blue shorts, a baggy navy T-shirt with a fat cartoon horse printed on it, and blue and white sneakers. She had light blond curls that bounced around her shoulders.

The woman was smiling, and her words came out in a rush. "Hello, dear," she said. "We're your neighbors." She pointed in the direction of their house. "I thought I should come over and introduce myself. I would have come over sooner, but we've been out of town. Is your mother home?"

Before I could reply, the woman pulled the blond girl forward.

"This is my daughter, Reese. You two look about the same age. Isn't that wonderful? I'm sure you'll be good friends in no time at all."

I smiled politely. I could see by Reese's annoyed expression that friendship wasn't exactly what she had in mind.

"I'm Annie. I'll get Mom," I told the woman, who still hadn't introduced herself. I stood aside from the doorway. "Please come in," I added.

I heard my mother's voice. "Annie! Is someone here? I thought I heard voices." Mom walked out of the kitchen.

Reese's mother smiled at my mother. "How nice to finally meet you," she said. "I'm Clara Moriarty. My daughter, Reese, was just getting to know your daughter. Her name is Annie, right?"

"That's right. And I'm Susan," my mother said. She seemed pleased by the unexpected visit. She invited Mrs. Moriarty to stay for coffee.

As Mom poured two cups of coffee, she said, "Why don't you take Reese to your room, Annie?"

Reese and I glanced at each other. We didn't really have a choice, so we left. Our mothers were already deep in conversation. My mom was so good at making friends.

Once inside my room, Reese looked around for a minute. Finally, she said, "I like your posters."

"Thanks," I said. "Look, about the other day —"

Reese shook her head to stop me. "Forget it. It was probably too much to expect that someone from the city would understand living in the country."

Her annoyed tone left me with nothing to say. Reese sighed. "I guess you'll learn, eventually," she said.

"What's that supposed to mean?" I asked, feeling insulted.

"Oh, nothing," she told me. "Whatever. Just forget it."

I wondered if I'd been kidding myself. How had I thought that I could ever be friends with such a rude girl?

I tried being friendly one more time. "Can't we just start over again? I did apologize. It would be easier if we could just get along, especially since we live next door to each other."

Reese was busily inspecting her fingernails. She shrugged and said, "Whatever."

Then our mothers walked into my room.

"Come on, Reese, time to go." Reese's mother looked at my horse posters. "Oh, another horse lover! How wonderful. I just knew you two would hit it off. I suppose Reese told you all about her horse. Reese has riding club tomorrow. I bet you would love to come along with us and get to meet everyone. Who knows! If you like what you see you may even want to join the club."

"Clara, that would be so nice," my mom said. "But Annie doesn't have a horse. And she doesn't know how to ride."

"I can too," I blurted out without thinking. "At least, I can ride a little."

Mrs. Moriarty didn't seem concerned about me not having a horse. "That settles it, then. Walk across the paddock in the morning. We're leaving at eight. You can be Reese's helper for the day."

The thought of being at Reese's beck and call all day didn't thrill me. Reese didn't look too excited about it either. But I couldn't think of a reason not to go, at least not without sounding rude.

"Thanks," I said. "I guess I'll see you at eight, then."

That night, I searched my wardrobe to find something that I could wear to a riding club. I didn't own a pair of jodhpurs. Besides, people might laugh at me if I came dressed as a rider when I wasn't actually riding.

But I didn't think it would be right to be too dressed up. I figured something casual would be fine.

Finally, I chose a pale pink tracksuit with blue stitching and a silver star on one shoulder. For a few months the previous year these outfits had been all the rage. Jade and I had matching tops. I finished off the outfit with my light blue running shoes.

The outfit wasn't really cool anymore, but judging by what Reese had been wearing, I didn't think fashion was a big deal here.

Early the next morning, I arrived at Reese's place. She was loading Jefferson into the horse trailer. Mrs. Moriarty smiled at me when I walked in, but quickly turned her attention back to Reese and Jefferson.

"Come on, Reese. Get that horse loaded right away, or we'll be late for gear check," Reese's mom said.

Reese rolled her eyes at me. "Mom gets a little tense on riding club days," she said.

"We have plenty of time. Usually we get there before anyone else arrives!"

Once Jefferson was safely tied in the trailer, the ramp closed up behind him. Reese and I climbed into the SUV.

Reese looked me up and down, and then raised her eyebrows. "Interesting outfit," she commented dryly.

I looked at Reese's outfit and then down at my own tracksuit. I had a sinking feeling that maybe I was wearing the wrong kind of clothes. Well, it was too late to do anything about it now.

Reese was wearing a tracksuit too, but hers was dark-colored and well-worn. Beneath Reese's jacket I saw a pressed white shirt and perfectly knotted necktie.

Reese was quick to notice my curious gaze. "It's part of the uniform," she told me. "If I didn't cover up, I'd be covered in dust by the time we got there."

When we arrived at the riding club, we were the first people to get there, just as Reese had told me we would be. It wasn't long before more cars and trailers rumbled through the gates one by one.

I looked around. It was like a scene from one of my favorite horse stories.

The riding club grounds were located in a large open space beside the Ridgeview racecourse. A square metal sign attached to the gate read "Ridgeview Riding Club." There were a couple of sheds and a long line of little grassy areas for horses.

Mrs. Moriarty backed the trailer up to one of the areas. In spite of Reese, I felt a rising excitement in my chest. A whole day to spend with horses. How perfect!

"I'll leave you girls to take care of Jefferson," Mrs. Moriarty said. "I need to get to the cafeteria." Then she headed off toward the sheds.

Reese jumped out of the car and went to open the ramp on the trailer.

"Annie, would you untie Jefferson?" Reese asked.

I stepped into the trailer through the side door and tried to untie the horse's lead rope. But I couldn't do it. The knot held fast, no matter what I tried. While I tried to loosen it, Jefferson stamped and fidgeted, shaking the horse trailer.

"He wants to get out," Reese called. "Hurry up, Annie."

"I can't get the knot undone." I was flustered. The more I struggled with the knot, the tighter it became.

Reese appeared at the door. She grabbed the end of the rope and pulled. I watched in frustrated amazement as the rope instantly and easily came undone.

"Okay, boy. Out you go," said Reese. The horse backed out slowly, one step at a time, until all four feet were off the ramp and back on solid ground. Jefferson looked around eagerly, announcing his arrival with a loud neigh.

I was mortified, but Reese gave me a wry smile. "It's a quick release knot," she explained. "I'll show you how to tie one if you want. Come on. We'll get him saddled up, and I'll take you to meet everybody else."

Before Reese brushed Jefferson she handed me a small can of black oil and a paintbrush. "You can oil his hooves," she said.

"What for?" I asked, realizing how dumb I sounded.

"It keeps them from drying out and splitting, especially in the dry weather. Plus, it makes them look nice. You really don't know much about horses, do you?" For once, Reese didn't make her words sound like an insult. She seemed to be just stating a fact.

I didn't reply. There didn't seem much point in denying the obvious.

Reese talked me through the process of oiling the horse's feet. I painted each of Jefferson's hooves with the black hoof polish until they gleamed. By the time I'd finished, my outfit was completely covered with black smears.

When I looked around, I saw that the grounds were bustling with activity. Adults were bringing equipment out from the sheds. Almost every yard had a horse in it, and all around us, people were busy getting their horses and ponies ready for the day.

Hellos rang out as friends greeted each other. A tall, fair-haired boy lugging a bucket of water stopped beside Reese as she positioned a saddle on Jefferson.

"Hi, Reese. Been riding much?" the boy asked. He offered me a polite smile.

"Nope, I've been out of town," Reese told him. "But I'll be riding a lot now. Austin, this is my new neighbor, Annie Boyd. She's here to check out the riding club."

Austin nodded. He looked at me a little oddly, and I could feel my face heating up. My pink tracksuit, covered with black oil stains, now seemed completely like the wrong thing to be wearing.

"Well, we can always use more members. I'll see you later." Austin moved on.

Embarrassed as I was, I was still really happy that Austin had assumed I was a rider.

I watched him walk down the line until he reached a very elegant-looking tall brown horse.

Reese followed my gaze. "Isn't Austin's horse pretty? Her name is Cruise. It's perfect for her. She's pretty laid back about most things. Austin needs a horse like Cruise. He takes his riding really, really seriously. He trains and he competes."

"Oh," I said. "Do you mean like at a show or something?"

Reese laughed. "No way," she said. "I'd like to see Austin Ryan at a show! No, he's into horse trials."

"Horse trials?" I repeated, mystified.

"You don't know the difference?" asked Reese, cocking her head.

"Um . . . no," I admitted.

"A horse trial is a competition where you ride a dressage test, then a cross-country course, and then a show-jumping course. You must have seen it on TV when the Olympics were on last year."

I smiled. I did remember seeing that, although it had all been a little confusing. "Of course, now I know what you mean," I said.

Reese had slipped Jefferson's bridle on as she spoke. Now she grabbed his reins and led him out of the yard. "Come on," she told me.

I took a deep breath and followed her. If the rest of these kids were anything like Reese, I was about to throw myself into the lion's den.

I followed Reese over to a small group of
people — a girl and two boys — that had
assembled near one of the sheds. They stood
holding their mounts and talking quietly. It
seemed like they were waiting for something or
someone.

I recognized Austin and his horse, Cruise.
All three riders wore their riding club uniforms.
Reese had removed her tracksuit, and now she
was in uniform too.

The riding uniform consisted of jodhpurs, brown riding boots, a white shirt and tie, and a safety vest. Some of the riders wore sweaters, too.

The two boys and Reese wore practical-looking white riding helmets on their heads. The other girl's helmet was a deep blue velvet that matched her sweater and tie perfectly. I felt their curious eyes scan me as I approached them.

"Everybody," Reese announced, "this is Annie, my new neighbor." Reese pointed to each person in turn. "Annie, this is Matt Snyder, Jessica Coulson — and you've already met Austin."

The guy named Matt Snyder held out his hand for me to shake. Compared to Austin, he wasn't tall. He had dark eyes and a welcoming grin. The top button of his shirt was undone, which made his tie hang crooked. A corner of his white shirt poked out from under his sweater.

"Nice to meet you," he said.

I held out a hand to pat Matt's horse. The animal pricked his ears and nuzzled my hand. "What a sweet horse," I said.

"His name is Bullet. And he's the fastest games horse in the west," said Matt. Bullet was solidly built, with every bit of him covered in speckly brown spots, from his broad rump to the tip of his muzzle.

"He's an Appaloosa, isn't he?" I asked.

"That's right," Matt replied. He grinned. He seemed pleased at my interest in his horse.

Reese stared at me in surprised amazement. "How did you know that?" she asked.

I shrugged mysteriously. "There are things about me you don't know," I joked.

The truth was, I had a large poster in my room at home of a horse that looked like Bullet. The caption on the bottom of the poster read, "Appaloosa — the horse with the spotted coat." But Reese didn't have to know that. I felt really good for getting something right for a change.

I smiled at Jessica, who stared back coldly without saying a word.

Jessica looked perfect. Not one stray hair escaped from beneath her fancy helmet. She was wearing expensive-looking suede gloves. She looked as if she'd just stepped out of one of my glossy horse magazines.

Jessica's horse was the most beautiful horse that I had ever seen. She was gleaming black all over, except for a shocking, perfectly white, diamond-shaped mark between her eyes. She was finely built, and her coat was spotlessly clean. She was just gorgeous.

To my surprise, Reese didn't seem bothered by Jessica's rudeness. "Jessica's horse is called Ripponlea Duchess," Reese explained patiently to me. "We usually just call her Ripple."

"She's beautiful," I said.

Then Jessica suddenly chimed in. "She should be," she said, tossing her head. "She cost a fortune. She's won Grand Champion Horse three times."

Before I could reply, a woman carrying a clipboard arrived.

"Good morning, everybody," she called out with a smile. "Are you all ready to be gear checked?"

Reese introduced me. "Mrs. Mason, this is my new neighbor, Annie," she said. "She's here to watch for the day."

"Welcome to Ridgeview Riding Club, Annie," Mrs. Mason said. "I'm the district commissioner for this club. Maybe we'll have a chance to talk later. Right now I need to get this group gear checked and starting their first lesson."

Mrs. Mason began to inspect the riders' gear. She began by looking at the bridles and saddles.

"What's she checking for?" I whispered to Reese while she waited for her turn to be checked.

"Everything," said Reese. "The gear check is for safety. The saddle has to be in good condition. If the leather cracks it can break. Loose stitching can come undone. You wouldn't want to be riding along and have your bridle or your stirrup leather suddenly break, would you?" Reese continued, "And everything should fit properly on the horse. Our horses have to carry us around all day. It's important that they're comfortable. Imagine if the saddle was rubbing or hurting his back all day. It would be horrible."

"I suppose it could be dangerous for the rider too," I said.

"That's right," Reese agreed, smiling a little. "A horse in pain could buck or rear up. A rider could be seriously hurt."

I was suddenly hopeful. It seemed to me that Reese was definitely thawing out. Her explanations were more patient now — less rude and sarcastic.

Mrs. Mason worked quickly. After checking the gear on the horses she inspected the riders, checking uniforms and making sure that helmets were correctly fitted and boots had proper soles for riding.

After each rider finally passed Mrs. Mason's gear check, they all mounted their horses. From my place on the sidelines, I could see that Jessica looked a little awkward getting into the saddle.

"What's the first lesson?" Jessica asked nervously.

"It's dressage first," Matt announced with a groan. "We don't get games today until the very last session."

"Jessica's worried." Speaking from Jefferson's back, Reese sounded slightly amused. "She's still a beginner and jumping scares her," she went on. "Good thing we have dressage first, right, Jess?" she said a little more loudly. "No need to worry."

Jessica shot Reese an unhappy look. "I'm not worried, and my name is Jessica," she snapped.

But Reese had already trotted off to the dressage arena. They all followed, leaving me to trail behind on foot.

I watched with interest while Reese's group rode their dressage lesson. The instructor was a woman named Erica. She seemed very strict to me, and she did a lot of yelling.

The riders rode around and around in a rectangular area. Mostly the horses were kept at a trot.

Erica seemed to have eyes everywhere. She noticed absolutely everything that each of the riders did.

"Matt, get those hands down right away," Erica called. "You're not riding in a bending race. I want to see that horse working on the bit. Jessica, sit UP and push your heels DOWN. That's good, Austin, she's going well. Reese, come on, that horse needs to be more FORWARD!"

After dressage, the riders had show jumping. A course of colorful show jumps had been set out. To me, the jumps looked high, but all the horses cleared them easily, until it came to Jessica's turn.

The instructor was an older man named Joe. When it was Jessica's turn, Joe dropped the jump down to a lower height. Even so, while the others cantered confidently and smoothly around and over each jump, Jessica kept Ripple trotting.

The very first time they approached a jump, Ripple stopped dead in front of it.

"She just won't go over," Jessica called to Joe.

"She will," Joe replied. "It's up to you as the rider to give her confidence."

Jessica looked frustrated. "She's too scared," she said.

"No, she's not," Joe said. "She can do it, if you help her."

It took a lot of encouragement, with many stops and starts, but after a while, Jessica and Ripple finally made it around the course. The sound of a whistle blowing echoed around the grounds.

"Lunch," Joe yelled. "Go and get it in the lunch shed."

The riders thanked him for the lesson. Then they headed back to the yards to unsaddle their horses.

In the shed, people had formed a line to buy food. Mrs. Moriarty was serving with another woman. When Jessica called the woman Mom, I began to understand a little more about Jessica.

Mrs. Coulson was the mirror image of her daughter. Compared to the other parents, who were all similarly dressed in old jeans and sweatshirts, Mrs. Coulson looked like she'd just stepped out of the pages of a fashion magazine.

I sat with Reese's group to eat my lunch. I hadn't realized how hungry I was until I started eating.

Must be all this fresh air, I thought. I wasn't used to spending so much time outside.

Between mouthfuls, the riders all discussed the morning's riding. No one paid much attention to me.

As I glanced around the room I noticed Matt talking to an older man. He wasn't much taller than Matt, but had the same dark eyes. I figured that the older man must be Matt's father.

Both of them had been looking in my direction. Matt said something and his father seemed to be nodding in agreement, but when they caught my eye they quickly turned away.

What was that all about? I wondered.

After lunch, I left Reese's group. I wandered over to where the junior group was riding a dressage lesson inside a rectangular, fenced arena.

There were a couple of gnarled old tree stumps jutting out of the ground at the far end. I chose one and sat down to watch the junior riders.

The horses were all small and shaggy, with bored expressions. They plodded patiently around the arena, looking as if they were used to the routine.

Erica was teaching the younger group. She was much easier on the younger ones than she'd been on Reese's group.

For a while it was fun to watch the concentration of the younger riders as they sat up tall and paid attention, as if learning to ride were the most important thing in the world.

There were three girls in this group. From listening to Erica talk to them, I figured out that their names were Natalie, Bree, and Sophie. I guessed that the girls were all probably around five years old.

But the skills of these riders were not developed enough to make for interesting viewing. I soon drifted off into a long daydream, where I rode my own horse at the riding club.

In my imagination, I rode well. Jessica, Austin, and even Reese were incredibly envious of me. I had the best horse, and everyone wanted to buy it from me.

The scene in my mind changed. I sat astride my wonderful horse in a show ring. I held a trophy in one hand and the reins in the other. A judge was placing a garland of flowers around my horse's neck. A man on a loudspeaker announced: "Annie Boyd has won the Grand Champion Rider event for the fourth time."

I was rudely jolted out of my daydream by a sharp stinging sensation on my leg. I looked down to see a thousand ants scurrying around the base of my tree stump. Oh no! It was just my luck to sit down right in the middle of an ant hill.

It really isn't fair, I thought as I jumped up and slapped myself around the legs. I was being forced to watch a bunch of spoiled brats who probably had no idea how lucky they were.

I was the one who had loved horses ever since I had first laid eyes on a performing circus horse when I was only three years old.

I was the one who should be here riding now, instead of having to be tortured by seeing everyone else with a horse to ride.

I realized I would never be happy to just sit and watch others ride. There had to be a way I could get my hands on a horse.

But how?

When I returned to Reese's group, they had joined some other riders and were practicing their skills at mounted games.

The groups were riding as teams, each of them lined up behind a big drum. Ahead of the drums were two lines of upright white poles spaced about three yards apart. The poles formed lanes, with another drum at the end of each line.

I stood on the sideline beside the instructor, the same man I had seen talking to Matt. He turned and spoke to me. "Hello, I'm Ray Snyder, Matt's father. I hear you're Rob Boyd's daughter. Annie, right?"

I had guessed right. This man was Matt's father. I was surprised to hear that Mr. Snyder not only knew who I was, but knew who my father was, too.

Mr. Snyder continued, "I bet you haven't met the senior group." He pointed to the line of riders beside Reese's group. "That's my older daughter, Laura, lined up first, then there's Georgie on the chestnut horse, Bryce on the paint, and Hannah on the white horse."

I nodded politely. The other group looked quite a bit older than Reese's group. I could see the family resemblance between Matt and Laura, although Matt was darker and more solidly built than his older sister.

Matt and Bullet were first in line for Reese's group. Bullet was misbehaving, bouncing up and down on the spot. He was obviously excited to get going. Matt didn't seem concerned. He sat confidently, lightly holding the horse in check.

Mr. Snyder held a flag up high. "Prepare to race," he called.

Matt brought Bullet under control. For a moment there was silence while riders and horses fell quiet, waiting for the start.

"Go!" Mr. Snyder called. He lowered the flag and the race was on.

Everyone began cheering madly as Matt expertly weaved Bullet in and out of the poles.

"Go, Matt," yelled Austin.

"Go, Laura," someone from the other team yelled.

Bullet streaked ahead of the rider in the other lane. He skidded around the end drum, leaning precariously, then raced back through the poles again. Matt went with him, glued to the saddle.

Jessica was next in line. She and Ripple traveled at a much slower pace, barely trotting. I saw Matt's face turn red with frustration as Jessica and her horse went along.

Before Jessica reached the drum, the other team had caught and passed her. I heard Matt groan loudly as he watched his giant lead disappear.

"Come on, Jess. Get her moving," Matt yelled.

But Jessica passed the line in her own good time, which was slow. That left Reese and

Austin with an impossible task to catch the new leaders in the next lane.

"Good one, Jessica," Matt said.

Matt's sarcasm didn't seem to bother Jessica, who made a face at him and trotted Ripple to the back of the line.

Mr. Snyder cut in. "Matt, behave yourself," he commanded. "Jessica is doing fine. You're part of a team, so show some team spirit. Besides, it's not a real race. We're practicing."

"Okay, Dad," Matt said. He nodded to his father, but rolled his eyes at me when Mr. Snyder wasn't looking. I couldn't help but chuckle. With Jessica's attitude, it was hard to feel sorry for her.

I thought the games were really cool. Reese and Jefferson put on a fine display through the poles, but then Austin made no effort to catch the leaders.

Cruise didn't seem to like the poles. She watched each one nervously and stayed as far away as possible from them.

As the pair came back past the drum, Mr. Snyder had something to say. "Austin, I know games aren't really your thing, but you could try a bit harder. It's good for you and your horse to learn new skills, you know."

Mr. Snyder's comments had little effect on Austin. He just shrugged and began heading back to unsaddle. The day's riding was done.

With the lesson over, Mr. Snyder turned his attention to me. "So, do you ride, young lady?" he asked.

I answered shyly. "I'd like to. But we just moved here. We're still settling in, really." I didn't want to tell Mr. Snyder that my father was the reason I wasn't riding, even if it was true.

"Well, we'd love it if you joined us here at the riding club. The lessons are a great way to learn," Mr. Snyder said. "But it's more fun to ride than to watch."

Mr. Snyder's words echoed in my ears on the short drive home. I had learned a lot, but standing around and watching others was already losing its appeal.

I wanted to join the riding club, but without a horse, I didn't see much point.

That was depressing. But at least Reese was in a good mood. The day at the riding club had left her much friendlier.

I was about to leave for the walk home when Reese stopped me. "Come over after lunch tomorrow," she told me. "Maybe you could try riding Jefferson."

Reese's idea was more than I could have hoped for, but I wasn't sure. After Reese's previous bad manners, I wondered if I could believe the offer was for real.

Then Reese added, "Look, Annie, I'm sorry I've been such a jerk. When your dog chased Jefferson, I was really mad. But I mean what I said about tomorrow. I'll give you a riding lesson. Will you come?"

I smiled. "I'd love to. I'll check with Mom and let you know."

"Great," Reese said. "See you then."

* * *

I jogged across the paddock and tore into the house. I was so excited to tell my mother I was going to get a riding lesson. But when I told her, my mother quickly ruined everything.

"Not tomorrow, Annie," she said. "We need to go into Ridgeview and buy books and a uniform for your new school."

I sighed. The last thing I wanted to do was think about school, even if it meant getting to go shopping.

"But, Mom, can't that wait?" I asked. "We've still got weeks and weeks until school starts."

"No, it can't wait," Mom said, shaking her head. "I don't want to leave it to the last minute and then find out things are unavailable just before you start school. I've set time aside to do it tomorrow, and that's when we'll do it. Besides, you love to shop. Maybe you can invite Reese to come with us."

Somehow, I knew that the last thing Reese would want to do was to tag along on a shopping trip.

Jade, on the other hand, would have loved it. Thinking of Jade gave me a hollow feeling in my chest. I missed Jade and decided to call her later that evening.

But right now what I needed was some air.

Just in case I felt hungry later, I grabbed an apple from the fruit bowl on the table and shoved it into my pocket for a snack. I told my mother I was taking Jonesy for a walk. Then I headed out the door.

Instead of taking my usual route into the woods, I turned right at the gate. I could stop at Reese's on the way back and explain about the shopping trip. Maybe Reese would offer to give me a riding lesson another time.

There were fewer houses this way and more open fields. There were acres of brown pastures. Grazing in most of them were small herds of cattle and a few sheep. I walked fast down the road, making Jonesy trot to keep up. In my mind, I replayed my day at the riding club.

Going to the riding club with Reese had made me want a horse more than ever. I decided to try talking to my dad again. If I told him all about the riding club, and how much fun it was, maybe I could somehow convince him to change his mind.

Besides, it came down to necessity. The only people I'd met so far were horse fanatics. How was I supposed to be happy if I was always the odd one out? I knew my parents wanted to see me fit in and make friends.

Of course! That was the perfect argument.

"That's it, Jonesy. I'll make him feel guilty," I said aloud.

Jonesy looked up at me and smiled in his doggy way. He waved his tail a couple of times to show me that he was listening.

The narrow, winding road climbed steadily into the hills. I had been walking for about half an hour and was thinking about turning around. Then I passed a driveway that led to a small green house. The house was old and rundown and it had a red roof.

What made the house stand out was the front yard. There must have been over a hundred rose bushes in full bloom. Every color imaginable filled the garden. I slowed down to look.

That's when I spotted the horse in the next paddock. He was standing under a big shady tree in a corner. He had his head down and one leg resting.

I forgot all about the roses. I bent down and picked up Jonesy. After the way he'd reacted to Reese's horse, I didn't want him barking and chasing this one.

Jonesy must have been tired, because he sat quietly in my arms without a wriggle or complaint.

The horse sensed my presence and raised his head sharply as I approached the fence.

"Hey, boy," I called softly.

The horse pricked his ears and took a few steps toward me, then stopped. He had a thick mane and tail and bright, curious eyes. His coat was a dark chestnut color all over. To me, he was magnificent, and I couldn't take my eyes off him.

"Come on," I coaxed. "Come here so I can pat you." The horse stared back at me with a calm expression, but he didn't move.

Jonesy was behaving himself, so I decided to take a chance and put him down. I slipped the end of the dog's leash around my wrist to make sure he couldn't get away from me — just in case.

I remembered the apple in my pocket. I pulled it out and leaned over the fence, holding the apple out to the horse. That got his interest. The horse walked right up to the fence and stretched his neck out, reaching to me for the apple.

I held out my hand with my palm up and the apple balanced on top. Once in the city park near my old apartment, a mounted police officer had shown me the correct way to offer food to a horse. The woman had told me that if I held the food flat on my palm, the horse couldn't bite me or accidentally catch my fingers in his teeth.

The horse grabbed the top half of the apple with his lips and bit into it. I was close enough to feel the horse's warm breath on my hand and smell his unique horse smell.

While he munched the apple, he allowed me to stroke his muzzle. Foamy apple juice mixed with horse saliva dribbled onto my sleeve.

I barely noticed. I stared into the horse's kind, toast-colored eyes and softly spoke.

"You could be mine," I said, wishing it were true. "You could teach me to ride. We could go to the riding club and learn about games, and dressage and jumping . . ." My words trailed away as I imagined myself on this coppery horse's back.

The horse nosed into my hand, searching for more food. When he didn't find any, he wandered off to graze, leaving me staring after him. I sighed and bent down to pick Jonesy up again. I held the dog close to me and turned for home.

When I returned to the house, my mother was speaking on the phone.

"Here she is. She just came in. Hold on." My mother handed me the phone with a happy smile. "It's Jade," she said.

I took the phone eagerly. "Jade! How did you know?" I said happily. "I was going to call you tonight."

"Sure you were," Jade teased.

Then she bombarded me with questions. "How's the new house? What's the town like? Are there any good stores? Have you made any new friends yet? Your mom said your new school year starts the same day as here. What do you think school will be like?"

I laughed. It was so good to hear Jade's voice. I told Jade all about the house and the town and the forest where I'd been taking Jonesy for walks.

I mentioned Reese, but I left out the fact that I'd spent the day at the riding club. I was hoping that Jade had forgotten about the horse I had so carelessly bragged about. The horse I didn't have.

It was all going well until Jade dropped the bombshell. "Guess what?" she said. "Your mom's been talking to my mom, and they said I can come and stay with you. We'll have a whole weekend together. I can't wait to see you — and your new horse, of course!"

I was speechless. I knew I should tell Jade that there was no horse, but all that came out was, "Um . . . yeah. I can't wait either."

Long after Jade hung up, I stood staring helplessly at the phone. Now I'd done it. Instead of finding a horse when she came, all Jade was going to find was that her good friend was a big fake.

I was standing half-dressed in a hot, airless changing room the next day when I suddenly remembered.

Oh no! I'd forgotten all about going to see Reese and Jefferson. As far as Reese knew, I was late for my riding lesson — by about two hours. I sighed. My neighbor was not going to be happy with me.

I wasn't happy either. Mom and I had discovered that shopping in Ridgeview was nothing like shopping in the city.

For one thing, there weren't many stores. And there wasn't much to buy at the stores there were.

We were inside Bartlett's Emporium — a run-down store with a paint-faded front that sold everything from underwear to camping goods. It was the only place in Ridgeview that sold school uniforms. I was used to the city, where the shopping choices were endless. Right now though, I had more urgent things to think about.

"Mom," I called to my mother outside. "Quick, pass me my phone."

My mother grumbled, "Why would you need your phone when you're trying on clothes?" But she passed the cell phone over the dressing room door.

I had to call information first to find out Reese's home number. When I was finally connected, Reese's mother answered.

"Annie," she said. "We were expecting you this afternoon."

"I'm so sorry, Mrs. Moriarty," I said. "I had to go out. Is Reese there?"

"Reese is outside unsaddling Jefferson," she told me. "She gave up on waiting for you and went for a ride."

I cringed at Mrs. Moriarty's cold tone. I felt terrible.

"Could you please tell Reese I'm sorry?" I said. "I meant to call and tell her last night that I couldn't make it today. I just . . . uh . . . forgot."

At this confession, Mrs. Moriarty sounded even more annoyed. "All right, Annie. I'll tell her. Goodbye."

I groaned. If Mrs. Moriarty was upset, and that seemed pretty obvious, imagine how Reese must feel. Great. I had ruined it completely.

I hadn't even been able to think up a decent excuse. I forgot? What a lame response. I must have sounded pathetic.

Reese would probably never speak to me again. Which meant I'd never learn to ride. *And*, I reminded myself, *you'll never have a friend in Ridgeview.*

My mother, unaware of the disaster, tapped on the door. "Hurry up, Annie. We still have to find school shoes."

By lunchtime, I was fully outfitted for life at my new school. I had a dress, a winter sweater and shirts, socks, shoes, a coat, and a rain jacket, all in the school colors of red, white, and charcoal gray.

For me, the whole experience was just a reminder of how soon the summer would be over. Then I would have to face starting from scratch at a new school.

When we were done shopping, we stopped at Ridgeview's one and only coffee shop and bakery, Coasters, and sat at a table for a late lunch.

A dark-haired woman, much older than my mom, came out from behind the counter to take our order.

"Afternoon, ladies," she said cheerily. "Are you here for lunch or just taking a nice coffee break?"

My mom launched into a long chat with the older woman. Sometimes the way my mother just latched on to people annoyed me. In just a few minutes my mother had introduced us both. Then she had told the woman all about shopping for school uniforms and that we were new in town and were living on the farm called Hillgrove.

"Well, isn't that a coincidence," replied the woman. "I happen to live out that way too, not too far from your place. I'm Marion Cameron, and I believe your husband and I are doing business."

"Of course!" said Mom, recognizing the name. "You have some sheep for us. Will they be available soon, do you think?"

"Not long now," Mrs. Cameron said. "The current batch of lambs will be yours as soon as they're big enough. That'll be in a couple of weeks." She turned her attention to me. "You'll have a bunch of young lambs to look after," she said kindly.

I was really annoyed now. The more I heard of the conversation, the angrier I became.

If it wasn't for the stupid sheep, I might be out buying a horse right now.

And if it wasn't for my mother making me shop today of all days, I would at least have been having a riding lesson instead of sitting in this bakery waiting for this woman to stop talking and take our order.

"I don't like sheep," I replied bluntly. "I actually think they're pretty disgusting."

That made my mother give me a dirty look. "Annie's a little disappointed," she told Mrs. Cameron, trying to make up for my rudeness. "She was hoping to have a horse now that we've moved away from the city. Her father thinks the sheep will be less trouble and take care of the grass, too. He's hoping Annie will learn to like the sheep."

"They're not the same as a horse," I said quietly.

Mrs. Cameron looked thoughtfully at me. "Hillgrove's a small farm; you wouldn't want to overstock it. But . . . " Mrs. Cameron tapped her fingers on the table as she spoke. "You would have room for a horse if you took a few less lambs."

I immediately felt bad. It wasn't this lady's fault that I didn't have a horse. I shot her a grateful look.

My mother laughed off the suggestion that we could have the sheep and a horse. "We'll see," she said. "Annie has quite a way to go to convince her father of that."

Mrs. Cameron chuckled. "Fathers can be stubborn at times. The trick is to put the thought in their heads and then let them think it was their idea," she said. "Good luck, young lady. And don't give up."

A few days later, as I clipped Jonesy's leash to his collar and prepared to leave for a walk, my thoughts turned to Reese. I had left three messages with Mrs. Moriarty but hadn't heard anything.

I debated with myself. I could go and apologize to Reese in person and risk making things even worse, or I could just lie low for a while, give Reese time to get over it, and then explain what happened.

But what if Reese didn't get over it? How long could we live next door to each other and not speak? And we would see each other at school. I didn't want an enemy at Ridgeview High before I even started school.

The truth was, I thought that Reese was overreacting. Was I going to have to keep apologizing forever? If Reese didn't call soon, I was just going to have to go over there and confront her.

Meanwhile, the horse down the road was fast becoming a new friend. The forest paths were forgotten now. Every day, I took an apple and walked Jonesy to the horse's corral. Now, at the sight of me, the horse came right up to the fence and nosed my pocket for his treat.

Today was no exception, but as usual he wandered off to graze when he finished his apple. But I wasn't ready to leave yet. I looked over at the house with the rose garden.

There was no movement — not a sign of anyone at home.

Hooking Jonesy's leash over the fencepost, I squatted down and squeezed myself between the fence wires. I'd almost reached the horse's side when I heard a shout. There was someone coming out of the house and walking toward me.

I panicked. I knew I shouldn't be on someone else's private property, and now I'd been caught red-handed. I could run, but by the time I got through the fence and collected Jonesy, I'd be caught.

I decided to stand my ground. Then I recognized the woman coming toward me. It was Mrs. Cameron, from the bakery.

I didn't know whether to feel relieved or not. Mrs. Cameron had seemed nice when I'd met her in the bakery, but I had been pretty rude.

As the woman approached, I began to try to explain. "Hello, Mrs. Cameron. I'm sorry . . . I . . . um . . . I just wanted to pat the horse, that's all. Really."

Mrs. Cameron was breathing quickly as she reached me. She carried a horse halter and rope in her hand.

"It's fine, dear. I've seen you from my window a couple of times," she said, "bringing old Bobby here an apple every day. I was just coming out to see if you'd like to catch him and brush him."

"That would be great," I said. "If you're sure it's okay."

Mrs. Cameron looked into my eyes. She smiled. Then she put her hands on her hips.

"Young lady, it's my belief that a horse needs a girl as much as a girl needs a horse," she said quietly. "Bobby is old, but he's not dead, and some attention would be good for him. He spends his time wandering around without any company."

Together, Mrs. Cameron and I walked to where Bobby was grazing. Mrs. Cameron handed the halter to me.

It took me a few minutes to figure out which part went where, but I had soon slipped the halter over Bobby's head.

I led Bobby through the gate. I was standing with the horse and Mrs. Cameron on the driveway when the horse's head shot up suddenly.

"What's the matter, Bobby?" she asked the horse. She glanced at me and added, "It's not like him to act like this. Something's bothering him."

Bobby was focused on the road, in the direction I had come from home.

Soon, we knew exactly what he was watching for. Thundering down the road in a pounding, out-of-control gallop, came Reese's horse, Jefferson.

Chapter Thirteen

Jefferson's hooves made sparks on the road as he galloped, the sound echoing in a frightening hammering rhythm. There was no sign of Reese. Jefferson's reins had come over his neck. The stirrups on his saddle flapped up and down, banging against the horse's sides.

I didn't know what to do. As the horse raced past us, Mrs. Cameron sprang into action. "That's Reese Moriarty's horse, isn't it?" she asked.

I nodded. Mrs. Cameron continued, "You take Bobby and follow that horse. He might calm down if he sees Bobby. When he stops, catch him and wait for me. I'm taking my car and going to find that poor girl. By the look of things, she must have fallen."

In minutes, Mrs. Cameron's car was zooming down the road and out of sight. I, who had never in my life been in charge of a horse on my own, had not been given time to explain or object.

"Well, Bobby," I said. "It's just you and me. Let's go find Jefferson." We set off in the direction Jefferson had headed.

Bobby walked at a lively pace beside me. He seemed as anxious to find Jefferson as I was. At first there was no sign of the runaway. But, as we went around a curve in the road, I heard a neigh. Bobby responded instantly with his own reply.

The horse's head was close to my ear, and I was startled by how loud it was.

Suddenly, there was Jefferson. He stood, head up with a nervous expression in his toast-colored eyes. My first reaction was relief to have found him, but then I looked down.

Jefferson had somehow managed to get his front legs caught in a coiled strand of loose wire. Jefferson tried to move toward Bobby and me, but with every movement the wire tightened around his legs.

"Whoa, boy," I whispered soothingly.

I held Bobby's rope in one hand and raised the other. I hoped Jefferson would think it was a calm gesture. Then, very slowly, I walked toward the trapped horse.

Talking softly to Jefferson, I reached out and stroked his hot, sweaty neck with my free hand.

I looked down to inspect the damage. A number of bloody patches on his legs showed where the hopelessly tangled wire had sliced the horse's skin.

I wanted to untangle the wire, but I had one hand holding Bobby, which made things difficult. Moving slowly so as not to startle Jefferson and entangle him further, I tied Bobby to the fence. The horses sniffed noses, each breathing in the other's scent. Bobby seemed to calm Jefferson down.

I bent down to Jefferson's legs. Working slowly, I gently began to uncoil the wire — bit by bit. I had to be extra careful. Jefferson flinched in pain whenever I had to pull hard to bring the wire away from his injured skin.

Finally, after what seemed like forever, I lifted the last section of the wire with my bloody hands. I didn't want to leave it on the ground. Some other animal could get tangled in it. So I hung the coil carefully over a fence post.

I untied Bobby. Then I picked up Jefferson's broken reins and, with a horse on either side of me, I headed for home. Despite Jefferson's injuries, he walked along just fine. That was a big relief.

I was almost back at Bobby's gate when Mrs. Cameron's car pulled up. Reese was sitting in the passenger seat. Her riding helmet was crooked. A long, dark stripe of dirt covered one side of her riding uniform. I figured that was where she must have fallen off and landed on the road.

Reese left the car and limped to where I stood with the two horses. She hugged Jefferson's neck.

"I found him tangled in wire. His legs are cut," I told her.

Mrs. Cameron got out of the car. "He'll be fine," Mrs. Cameron told Reese, looking at Jefferson's legs. "He'll need a tetanus shot to prevent infection, and I'd put some iodine on those wire cuts if I were you. There might be some swelling, but the wire didn't go in deep. Give him a week off to rest, and he'll be right as rain."

"Thanks so much for catching him, Annie," Reese said. "I was so worried. He could have been hit by a car or . . . well . . . anything could have happened." Reese shuddered and hugged Jefferson again.

I asked Reese, "What about you? Are you okay?"

Reese looked embarrassed and rubbed her thigh. "I landed on my leg. It wasn't Jefferson's fault. There was a rabbit. It came out from behind a tree, and Jefferson got freaked out. I kind of lost my seat and went backwards. I accidentally kicked him in the flanks. That's what made him run." She added sheepishly, "I was daydreaming. If I'd been paying attention, none of it would have happened."

I nodded. I was pretty surprised. Reese and her friends had made it all look so easy at the riding club. I was beginning to realize that riding might be more of a challenge than I thought.

Once Bobby had been returned home, Reese and I said goodbye to Mrs. Cameron. Then we walked home together.

I tried to apologize for the missed riding lesson, but Reese cut me off.

"Forget it. Mom told me you called. I understand." She paused. "Hey, are your hands okay?" she asked.

I held up my hands. "Jefferson's blood, not mine," I explained.

Reese shuddered again. "Maybe we can reschedule that lesson when Jefferson's legs are healed," she said.

I brightened. "I'd love to. And I promise I'll show up this time."

"Hey, just make sure you don't wear that pink tracksuit," suggested Reese with a frown.

I got the giggles. After a moment, Reese joined in.

A few days later, I waited nervously for Jade to arrive with her mother. At the sound of a car engine coming up the driveway, I flicked back my bedroom curtains and peered out my window for the fourth time that morning.

It must be them, I thought. I was really excited to see my friend, but I was dreading the moment when I would have to tell Jade the truth. There was no horse and never would be. And sheep just weren't going to make up for that.

I took one last look in the mirror. My outfit — jeans, sneakers, and a dark-colored sweatshirt — was simple and plain. Jade would probably think my outfit was kind of boring, but I had learned a thing or two about country life. It paid to dress practically.

But when I ran outside, I saw that it wasn't Jade. Standing in the yard, talking to my mother and father, was Mr. Snyder, from the riding club.

My dad introduced me. "Annie," he said, "this is my boss at Ridgeview Real Estate, Ray Snyder."

Mr. Snyder laughed, holding his hand out for me to shake. "We've met, actually," he explained. "Annie spent a day as a guest at my son's riding club."

"She did?" my father asked. He looked bewildered.

"Don't you remember, Rob? She went with the Moriartys, from next door," my mother explained.

"Uh . . . um . . . oh yes," my father said.

I tried to hide a giggle. It was obvious that my father didn't remember at all.

Mr. Snyder and my father excused themselves and went inside to talk business. A white station wagon drove in and parked beside the house. This time it really was Jade and her mother in the car.

Jade jumped out of the car wearing an enormous grin. We squealed with delight and ran to hug each other.

Mrs. O'Brien followed more calmly, carrying a box of cookies in her arms.

"Annie," she said. "Make some coffee. I have homemade cookies and the smell has been torturing Jade since we left home. All I ask in return is a nice hot cup of coffee."

We all trooped into the house. Dad introduced Mrs. O'Brien to Mr. Snyder. Then the adults sat down for cookies and coffee.

Armed with a handful of chocolate cookies, I grabbed Jade by the arm and took her on a tour of the house.

I left my own room for last. Jade glanced quickly around the room but didn't seem too interested.

"So where is it?" she asked bluntly.

"Where's what?" I replied.

"The horse, of course. I'm dying to see him. Or is it a her?"

"Jade, I —"

A loud hiss of truck brakes interrupted my explanation.

"Well, now, who could that be?" I heard my father ask from the kitchen.

Everyone headed outside. Parked in the driveway was a large truck with a stock crate on the back.

Mrs. Cameron was driving the truck. She waved at us, but no one was looking at her. All eyes were on the back of the truck.

Standing in the back of the truck were six of the oddest-looking animals that I had ever seen. I realized that they must be the sheep my father had ordered. They had short, close-to-the-skin coats instead of thick wool. They had floppy ears and long curled horns. These animals didn't look like sheep at all. They looked more like some kind of exotic mountain goat.

But the sight of these odd-looking, goatish sheep was not the cause of my amazement. Standing with the sheep, looking around curiously, and completely out of place, was Bobby.

Mrs. Cameron backed the truck up to the paddock gate outside my bedroom and turned off the motor. Still beaming, she jumped down from the truck cab and began to lower the ramp at the back, ready to unload the animals.

"Hello, all," she said. "One delivery of sheep as ordered."

But my father did not look impressed. "Uh, Mrs. Cameron," he said. "I believe I ordered eight sheep. There are only six here. And I don't remember ordering a horse!" He pointed in the direction of the crate.

"Yes, you're right," said Mrs. Cameron. "There was a little problem with supplying eight sheep. I could only get the six. However, I believe you wanted the sheep to keep the grass short. So I decided to throw in this old horse here. He'll earn his keep by eating enough grass for two sheep, I bet."

I glanced at Jade. She looked confused, trying to follow the thread of the conversation. Then I looked from Mrs. Cameron to my own mother. Both wore innocent expressions. I was sure that they weren't as innocent as they looked.

My father was trying to stay polite but firm. "That's very kind of you, Mrs. Cameron. But I really don't want a horse. I guess six sheep will be enough. You can take the horse back with you."

By now the sheep had filed down the ramp and streamed into the paddock. Bobby, tied up, stayed on the truck. Mrs. Cameron ignored my dad and gestured to me. Then she waved her hand in the direction of the horse.

"Annie," she said. "Climb up and lead him out for me."

I looked hopefully in my father's direction, but I was afraid to move. Everything was happening so fast. I resisted the rising excitement I felt. I knew my father was never going to agree to this.

"I don't think —" my father began.

But he was interrupted by Mr. Snyder. "You know, Rob," Mr. Snyder said, "that old horse would be perfect for Annie. He'll teach your daughter to ride. And we're always looking for new members at the riding club. Riding is a great sport, you know. It would be an excellent way to get Annie involved in her new community."

Then Mom spoke. "That's true, Rob. Joining a club will help her to settle in and make friends."

My father looked around him at four expectant faces and sighed. "Something tells me I'm being tricked," he said.

Then he looked at me. I was holding my breath, hardly daring to hope.

"Go ahead, kiddo," he said gruffly. "Go and untie your horse."

In a flash, I was up on the truck and leading Bobby down the ramp.

"He's your problem, Annie, and your responsibility," my father added.

I could hear my father's voice, but my senses were far too absorbed by the horse beside me to pay any attention to my dad. I could feel Bobby's warmth beside me and smell his delicious horsey smell. He was real. And he was mine!

But the look on Jade's face cut through my happiness. My friend had turned pale and was really quiet. Something was bothering her.

"What is it, Jade? What's wrong?" I asked my friend.

I was shocked when Jade burst into tears.

"Oh, Annie," she sobbed. "I feel so bad. I was so upset when you had to leave the city. And you didn't seem sad or anything. It seemed like you were happy to go off and make a bunch of new friends and leave me behind. And that story about you getting a horse — well, I thought you were . . . I thought you were just showing off. I thought you made the whole thing up. I'm so sorry. Can you forgive me?"

I really wanted to clear things up with Jade. But first there was something important that I needed to do.

I grabbed Jade's shoulders and squeezed gently. "Jade," I said. "I'm the one who should be feeling bad. Of course I hated leaving. I especially hated leaving you. And that whole horse thing . . . I can explain. Just hold on. I'll be back. Just give me a minute."

Mrs. Cameron closed up the ramp on the truck and climbed back into the driver's seat. I ran to say goodbye, but as I reached the window, I was suddenly shy. I didn't know how I could ever thank her for such a wonderful gift.

Mrs. Cameron spoke first. She had to yell loudly to be heard over the truck's engine. "You have fun with that horse, okay?" she said.

I nodded. My eyes stung with tears. "I'll take good care of him, I promise," I finally blurted. "Thank you so much."

"Oh, I know you'll be good to him," said Mrs. Cameron in a tone that told me she never had any doubts. "And in turn, Bobby will teach you everything you need to know. So be sure to pay attention."

Mrs. Cameron shifted the truck into gear and drove off down the driveway.

I settled Bobby into his new home. I gave him a pat and showed Jade how to stroke his soft muzzle.

"I hope you're going to be happy here, Bobby," I whispered.

Bobby seemed to be the only one that wasn't surprised by the turn of events. He bobbed his head, and then ignored the sheep as he busily explored the grazing in his new paddock.

"He's beautiful, Annie," said Jade. "You're so lucky."

"You have no idea," I said. "Jade, let me tell you the real story about my new horse, Bobby."

About the Author

When she was growing up, Bernadette Kelly desperately wanted her own horse. Although she rode other people's horses, she didn't get one of her own until she was an adult. Many years later, she is still obsessed with horses. Luckily, she lives in the country, where there is plenty of room for her four-legged friends. When she's not writing or working with her horses, Bernadette and her daughter compete at riding club competitions.

Horse Tips from Bernadette

- Never ride alone.

- A frightened horse is a dangerous horse. Stay calm around your horse.

- Horses need food for energy. But overfeeding your horse is just as bad as underfeeding it. Keep your horse healthy.

- Learn everything you can about horses.

For more, visit Bernadette's website at
www.bernadettekelly.com.au/horses

Glossary

- **acre** (AY-kur)—a measurement of an area equal to 43,560 square feet (about the size of a football field)

- **corral** (kuh-RAL)—a fenced area for animals

- **dressage** (dress-AHJ)—the art of riding and training a horse

- **encounter** (en-KOUN-tur)—an unexpected or difficult meeting

- **flanks** (FLANGKS)—the sides of an animal, between its ribs and hips

- **jodhpurs** (JOD-purz)—pants worn for horseback riding

- **mortified** (MOR-tih-fyed)—embarrassed

- **neutral** (NOO-truhl)—pale, not colorful

- **opportunity** (op-ur-TOO-nuh-tee)—a chance to do something

- **outskirts** (OUT-skirts)—the outer edges of a place

- **paddock** (PAD-uck)—an enclosed area where horses can graze or exercise

Advice from Annie

Dear Annie,

I recently moved to a new town. I don't have any friends here, and it's really different from where I used to live. What can I do to make sure I'm not totally miserable?

Sincerely,

Friendless in Fremont

Dear Friendless in Fremont,

Don't worry! It takes time to make new friends. I know it seems hopeless right now, but before long, you'll feel just as comfortable in your new town as you did in your old one.

Here are some ways to make friends:

1. **Be outgoing.** You won't meet friends inside your house, so even if you're scared, make an effort to get out there.

2. **Be creative.** Think about your interests. Join a club or group that shares your likes. If you can't find one, start one!

3. **Be friendly.** Introduce yourself to your neighbors, smile at other girls your age at the mall, and wave to people you see walking down your street.

4. **Be brave.** If you meet a new friend, don't be afraid to call her and invite her over.

No matter what, don't give up! Your new friends are out there. Keep looking, and you'll find them!

Love,
♡ Annie

The Ridgeview Book Club Discussion Guide

Use these reading group questions when you and your friends discuss this book.

1. Talk about Annie's father. What do you think about the way he treats Annie? What could she do to change their relationship?

2. Annie's dream is to own a horse of her own. Luckily, she meets Bobby. If she hadn't, what are some ways she could have made her dream come true? Discuss pros and cons of each path she could have taken on her way to owning a horse.

3. When Annie moves to Ridgeview, she leaves her best friend, Jade, behind in the city. Talk about this. How would you feel if you left your best friend? What would you do to make sure your friendship stayed strong, even if you weren't living in the same place and going to the same school?

The Ridgeview Book Club Journal Prompts

A journal is a private place to record your thoughts and ideas. Use these prompts to get started. If you like, share your writing with your friends.

1. Write about your biggest dream. What is it? Why is it so special? Do you think it will ever come true, and why or why not? How could you make your dream come true?

2. Make a list of attributes you look for in your friends. Next, make a list of attributes about yourself. Finally, make a list of attributes you don't want in a friend. Where do the lists overlap? Where are they different?

3. Relationships with parents can be very complicated. Write about a time when you and your parents had an argument. What happened? How did you resolve it? Then write about a happy time you spent with your family. What made it a good time?

Join the Ridgeview
Riding Club!

Read all of Annie's
adventures.

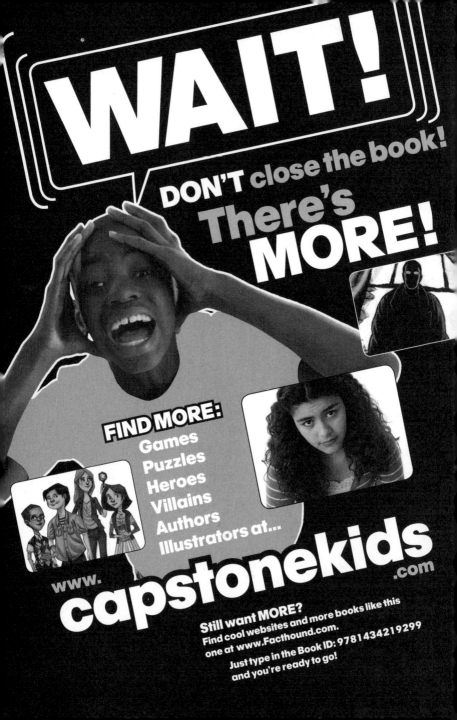